THE DEPARTMENT OF JUSTICE

A LOOK BEHIND THE SCENES

By Michael Burgan

Content Consultant:
Kevin Boyle, JD
Professor, School of Public Affairs
American University
Washington, D.C.

COMPASS POINT BOOKS
a capstone imprint

Compass Point Books are published by Capstone
1710 Roe Crest Drive, North Mankato, Minnesota 56003
www.mycapstone.com

Library of Congress Cataloging-in-Publication Data
Names: Burgan, Michael, author.
Title: The Department of Justice : a look behind the scenes / by Michael Burgan.
Description: North Mankato, Minnesota : Compass Point Books, 2019. | Series: U.S. government behind the scenes | Includes bibliographical references and index.
Identifiers: LCCN 2018042025 (print) | LCCN 2018042871 (ebook) | ISBN 9780756559168 (ebook PDF) | ISBN 9780756559038 (hardcover) | ISBN 9780756559120 (pbk.)
Subjects: LCSH: United States. Department of Justice—Juvenile literature. | Justice, Administration of—United States—Juvenile literature.
Classification: LCC KF5107 (ebook) | LCC KF5107 .B868 2019 (print) | DDC 347.73—dc23
LC record available at https://lccn.loc.gov/2018042025

Editorial Credits:
Amy Kortuem, editor; Terri Poburka, designer; Jo Miller, media researcher Tori Abraham, production specialist

Image Credits:
AP Images: Ben Earp, File, 8; Getty Images: Bettmann/Contributor, 33, Bloomberg/Contributor, 11, Boston Globe/Contributor, 36, David Hume Kennerly/Contributor, 29, 35, Eliot Elisofon/Contributor, 38; Newscom: Jeff Malet Photography, 55, Reuters/Stringer, 14, UPI/Roger L. Wollenberg, 5, ZUMA Press/Ron Sachs, 31, ZUMA Press/Shane T. Mccoy, 24; Shutterstock: bakdc, 47, Everett Historical, 20, fitzcrittle, 6, GagliardiImages, 57, JPL Designs, 7, sebra, Cover; Wikimedia: FBI, 27, 41, LOC/Harris & Ewing, 39, LOC/MarionS. Trikosko, 25, NARA, 43, NARA/Okamoto, Yoichi R. (Yoichi Robert) Photographer, 23, United States Department of Justice, 48, 53

Design Elements:
Shutterstock: anndypit, ben Bryant, RetroClipArt, Tobias Steinert

Printed and bound in the USA.
PA49

TABLE OF CONTENTS

CHAPTER ONE

Justice for All

Growing up in Florida during the early 2010s, Steve Mack had a tough childhood. He spent time in several foster homes before moving in with his grandmother. As a teen he began using drugs and was arrested for stealing. Instead of sending him to jail, a judge sent Mack to a residential commitment program. The focus of the program is to help troubled teens get any needed medical treatment, as well as counseling for emotional issues. The goal is to help the teens avoid committing more serious future crimes and perhaps going to prison.

Palm Beach County had worked with several nonprofit groups to set up the program. While in the program, Mack learned about a service in his county called Back to a Future (BTAF). Mack probably didn't know that BTAF was supported by the massive federal agency that fights crime in many ways across the country. BTAF helps prepare teens like Mack to move out of residential commitment programs and return to daily life. The BTAF staff helped Mack prepare for college. "I started seeing a whole bunch of open doors," he said. When he was released, he was the first of his friends to go to college.

To start BTAF in 2013, Palm Beach County received federal money under the Second Chance Act. Congress passed the law in 2008. It sets aside money for grants given to state, local, and tribal governments, as well as to nonprofit groups. The program gave out $68 million in 2017 and has given about $300 million since it began.

Enforcing Justice

The Second Chance Act Grant Program is operated by an office of the U.S. Department of Justice (DOJ). It is just one part of the department's efforts to reduce crime in the United States. The DOJ fights crime directly. It can take evidence gathered from agencies such as the Federal Bureau of Investigation (FBI) and prosecute people accused of breaking the law. The department also fights crime

President George W. Bush signed the Second Chance Act in 2008 to help former criminals become successful citizens.

A Florida teen demonstrated at the March for Our Lives rally in Tampa, Florida, in 2018.

indirectly through programs like the Second Chance Act. But the department has a wide range of other duties. The DOJ helps make sure that all Americans are guaranteed the right to vote. It also keeps track of the conditions in prisons to make sure prisoners are not mistreated.

Department officials also have a role in deciding how to enforce certain laws or interpret what an executive order means. These orders are made by presidents on many issues. In 2017, for example, President Donald Trump issued one to limit immigration from certain nations into the United States. He argued this was necessary to reduce the threat of terrorism in the country. Afterward, an office within the Justice Department gave legal approval to the order.

Under the system of government outlined in the U.S. Constitution, the president is in charge of the executive branch. The executive is one of three branches in the federal government. Congress is the legislative branch—it proposes laws for the country. As the head of the executive branch, one of the president's duties is to approve or reject those laws. The third branch, the judicial, interprets laws. It carries out trials when people are accused of breaking federal laws. Some federal courts also hear appeals of decisions made by the country's district courts. The U.S. Supreme Court is at the top of the judicial branch. It can determine if a law violates the Constitution and should be overturned.

The Department of Justice is one of 15 departments in the executive branch of the U.S. government. The heads of each of those departments form part of the president's cabinet. They are the top advisors he or she turns to when deciding what policies to pursue. Although part of the executive branch, the DOJ works closely with federal courts. The department is in charge of enforcing federal laws and prosecuting people accused of breaking them. In the U.S. legal system, there are both state and federal courts. The DOJ generally is not involved in state court actions.

Twenty-one-year-old Dylann Roof was sentenced to life in prison after killing nine people in a Charleston, South Carolina, church in 2015.

At times, though, federal and state laws might both come into play when a crime is committed. For example, in 2015 a white man named Dylann Roof killed nine black people in a Charleston, South Carolina, church. He was charged by the state with murder. The federal government charged him separately with committing a hate crime. He had admitted targeting his victims because of their race and his hatred of African Americans. In cases like that, state and federal prosecutors argue the case in separate courts.

Top Lawyer

The head of the Department of Justice is the U.S. attorney general (AG). The attorney general directs the operations of the department and represents the United States in legal matters. The attorney general also gives legal advice and opinions to the president, the president's cabinet, and the heads of other executive branch agencies. Part of the president's duties is appointing federal judges and people to fill certain positions within the Department of Justice. The attorney general recommends people who are best qualified for these jobs.

Within the DOJ, the attorney general and his or her top aides direct such important law enforcement agencies as the Drug Enforcement Administration and the Bureau of Alcohol, Tobacco, Firearms, and Explosives. Perhaps the best known of the department's criminal investigators are the agents of the Federal Bureau of Investigation. Long ago, they were nicknamed "government men"—G Men for short. Over the years, they have tracked down murderers and kidnappers, arrested spies, and sought to prevent terrorist attacks. Other DOJ offices and agencies address other issues such as tax evasion, and enforce laws that affect the environment and violence against women.

The Country's Lawyer, Not the President's

When describing the attorney general as the top lawyer for the United States, some people think this means he or she is also the lawyer for the president. In reality, U.S. presidents have their own attorney, known as the White House Counsel. This lawyer advises the president and White House staff on legal issues related to the president's role as the chief of the executive branch. In some cases, presidents might also name a lawyer called a special counsel to focus on a specific legal issue related to the presidency. In 2017 Donald Trump named Ty Cobb a special counsel. Cobb's duty was to address the White House's response to the investigation of possible ties between members of Trump's 2016 presidential campaign and the Russian government. In 1994 President Bill Clinton hired Jane Sherburne as a special counsel when Clinton faced legal questions about some of his activities before and after he was elected president. Presidents also have personal attorneys who represent them if they face legal issues not related to their public duties.

President Trump and his cabinet discussed immigration policy during a cabinet meeting in June 2018.

Another important task for the attorney general is supervising the legal representation of the federal government in cases that go to the U.S. Supreme Court. While attorneys general can argue these cases themselves, the job usually falls to another person in the DOJ, the solicitor general. The solicitor general takes on most cases before the Supreme Court so the attorney general can focus on his or her many other responsibilities. The attorney general also directs how the government will present its cases involving the United States in other courts.

For federal law cases, the United States is divided into 94 districts, and each has a district court. There are district courts in every state, with some states having two or more. The District of Columbia, Puerto Rico, and the U.S. Virgin Islands each make up separate districts. The territories of Guam and the Northern Mariana Islands are also separate districts, but they share one U.S. attorney. This adds up to 93 attorneys. The U.S. attorneys for each district prosecute both criminal and civil cases related to federal law. The attorney general oversees the actions of the district attorneys.

Helping the attorney general with that task is the deputy attorney general, the department's second-in-command. The president also chooses the person for this position. The U.S. Senate must approve this choice. The deputy attorney general works closely with the attorney general to run the department, having direct day-to-day control more than 25 offices and agencies within the DOJ. The 93 U.S. attorneys also report directly to the deputy AG. The deputy attorney general has the same power and authority as the attorney general, unless a law specifies that only the attorney general or another department official has the power to carry out a certain action.

America's Attorneys

The 93 U.S. attorneys are a key part of the Department of Justice and the federal judicial system. As with the attorney general and the top two assistants in the department, the president chooses lawyers to serve as U.S. attorneys. Then the Senate must approve the choice. Once confirmed, U.S. attorneys hold their position for four years, though the president can ask that they leave sooner. Individual senators often play a role in selecting the candidates for these positions. Traditionally, the senators from the state in which the judicial district lies must approve the person the president chooses before the entire Senate votes to give its approval. This is known as the "blue slip process." The home-state senators mark their approval or rejection on a slip of blue paper.

Once confirmed in their jobs, U.S. attorneys work with assistant attorneys. The assistant attorneys are hired by the U.S. attorneys, usually after they have already gained experience in either civil or criminal law. After they serve for four years, attorneys volunteer to resign their positions. The president may ask serving attorneys to remain on the job. If the president is from a different political party than the one that previously controlled the executive branch, he or she is likely to accept all the resignations. That allows them to appoint new attorneys who share their political beliefs.

Justices Ruth Bader Ginsburg (left), Samuel Alito (center), and Elena Kagan (right) heard arguments during a Supreme Court case in 2013.

One specific duty of the deputy attorney general is representing the Department of Justice at White House meetings on national security and terrorism. Another is authorizing the government to secretly collect some forms of intelligence. The deputy AG recommends whether or not the federal government should seek the death penalty as the punishment for certain crimes. The deputy also helps the president decide whether or not someone should receive a pardon for a crime or if a sentence given by a federal court should be reduced. The president's power to pardon, or forgive, a crime is spelled out in the Constitution. The U.S. Supreme Court has interpreted that to mean presidents can also reduce a sentence.

Just below the deputy attorney general is the associate attorney general. The person in the DOJ's number-three position helps both the AG and deputy AG carry out their duties. The associate AG has the job of supervising the work of several divisions in the department, including the ones that deal with laws relating to taxes and the environment. Working with the deputy AG, the associate AG also oversees the Office of Tribal Justice, which deals with legal relations between the U.S. government and American Indian tribal nations.

While the attorney general and his or her two top aides are often in the public eye, the Department of Justice relies on the hard work of almost 110,000 people to carry out its work. The department's mission is, "To enforce the law and defend the interests of the United States according to the law; to ensure public safety against threats foreign and domestic; to provide federal leadership in preventing and controlling crime; to seek just punishment for those guilty of unlawful behavior; and to ensure fair and impartial administration of justice for all Americans."

Who Does What at the DOJ

Attorney General (AG)
Oversees the entire department and represents the United States in some legal cases

Associate Attorney General (ASG)
Helps the AG and DAG; manages several divisions and works with the DAG on issues of tribal law

Deputy Attorney General (DAG)
Assists the AG by overseeing 25 divisions within the department and managing the 93 U.S. attorneys; works with the White House on issues of terrorism and intelligence

Solicitor General (SG)
Represents the U.S. government in most legal cases, so the AG has more time for other duties

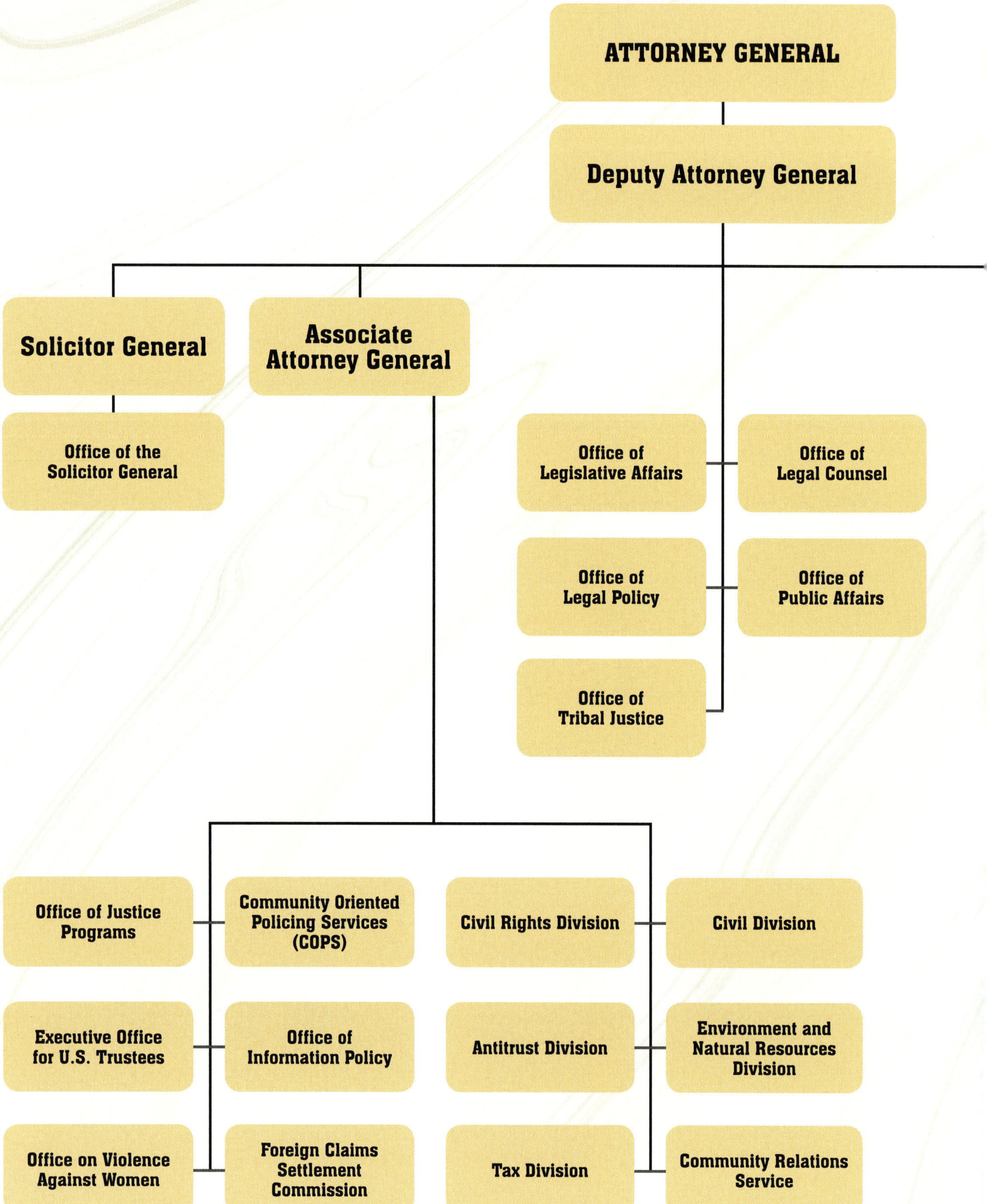
ATTORNEY GENERAL
Deputy Attorney General
Solicitor General
Associate Attorney General
Office of the Solicitor General
Office of Legislative Affairs
Office of Legal Counsel
Office of Legal Policy
Office of Public Affairs
Office of Tribal Justice
Office of Justice Programs
Community Oriented Policing Services (COPS)
Civil Rights Division
Civil Division
Executive Office for U.S. Trustees
Office of Information Policy
Antitrust Division
Environment and Natural Resources Division
Office on Violence Against Women
Foreign Claims Settlement Commission
Tax Division
Community Relations Service

Organizational Chart

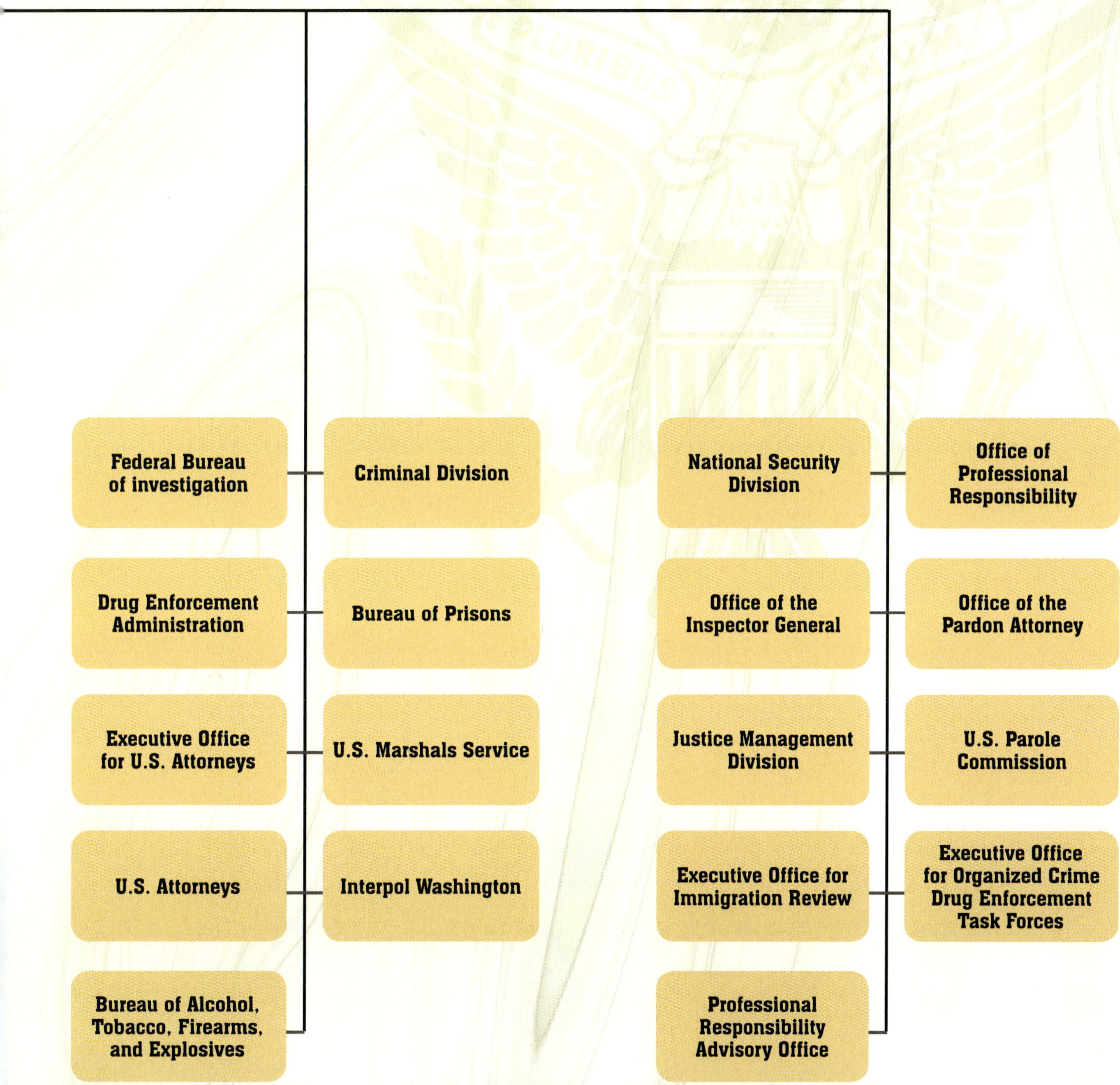

CHAPTER TWO

Creating and Building the Department of Justice

In 1787 representatives from 12 of the original 13 states met in Philadelphia to discuss the powers and structure of the federal government in their young nation. (Rhode Island did not take part because its representatives feared a stronger government might pass laws that would harm its economy.) The goal was to create a strong national government for the new United States. It had just won its independence from Great Britain. However, it had only a weak central government that left most powers to the separate states. In Philadelphia the representatives wrote the U.S. Constitution, which was the structure of this new government.

The Constitution created the three branches of the federal government. But it did not specify how the executive branch should be set up. The writers of the Constitution left that to Congress to decide. They also let Congress create federal courts below the Supreme Court.

In the summer of 1789, members of the first Congress passed the Judiciary Act. President George Washington signed it into law that September. Among other things, the act called for the creation of three circuit courts and 13 district courts. Circuit courts heard most trials involving federal law. District courts took cases dealing mostly with law involving shipping. Each district also had an attorney who would represent the government in legal cases.

The Judiciary Act spelled out in detail the duties of the new courts and the judges appointed to them. It ended by calling for the creation of the position of attorney general. The idea of having one lead attorney to represent the government's interests went back to Great Britain. Since the 15th century, that country's kings and queens had someone with the title of attorney general presenting their side of legal arguments. The Judiciary Act said the U.S. attorney general had to be "learned in the law" and would "prosecute and conduct all suits in the Supreme Court in which the United States shall be concerned, and to give his advice and opinion upon questions of law when required by the President of the United States, or when requested by the heads of any of the departments."

Washington chose Edmund Randolph as the first attorney general. Writing to him, Washington said, "I have considered the first arrangement of the Judicial department as essential to the happiness of our Country, and to the stability of its political system." Although Washington wrote "Judicial department," he was really talking about the judicial branch of the government. Congress would not create the Department of Justice for another 81 years.

Randolph had studied law in Virginia, where several members of his family had served as attorney general when it was a British colony. During the American Revolution, he was elected to the Continental Congress. It served as the national government for the states during the war. For a time Randolph was Virginia's attorney general. Later, as governor of his home state, he took part in the convention that wrote the Constitution.

Although he didn't lead an executive department, Randolph was a member of Washington's cabinet. At first the cabinet had just four people: the heads of the Treasury, State, and War departments, and the attorney general. Washington didn't hold his first cabinet meeting with all four until 1791. These meetings were not held regularly until 1793.

Randolph's powers and duties were limited. Unlike today, he and the AGs who followed him over the next few decades didn't have authority over the U.S. attorneys. Randolph asked for that power and Washington supported him. Congress, however, did not go along with the idea. Randolph didn't have staff to help with his duties,

Edmund Jennings Randolph was appointed the nation's first attorney general in 1789 by President George Washington.

either. He turned to Congress again, asking for a law that would give him a clerk. The move failed. It took almost 30 years for Congress to give the attorney general a clerk. The first attorneys general didn't even have their own government offices.

Congress also paid Randolph less than the other cabinet members. That led him to practice law for people outside the government so he could make money. Until 1853 attorneys general were still paid less than the heads of the executive departments. All had to rely on their private legal businesses to add to their incomes. Some did not even live in Washington, D.C., so they could work in their private practices in their hometowns.

After Andrew Jackson was elected president in 1828, he asked Congress to give the attorney general more authority. The lawmakers refused. Each department had its own lawyers, instead of the attorney general overseeing them. Most of the responsibility to carry out federal law cases went to the Department of the Treasury, which oversaw the work of the U.S. attorneys.

The Beginnings of the Department of Justice

From Jackson's presidency through the 1850s, some government officials talked about creating a separate Department of Justice. Congress opposed it. Some lawmakers were not in the same political party as the president. They did not want the president creating new jobs for his party's members. Some officials in the Treasury Department did not want to lose the role they had overseeing U.S. attorneys in the judicial process.

By the start of the Civil War in 1861, the attorney general was working for the federal government full time. The war itself led to a rise in federal legal cases. New laws passed during the war led to taxes on liquor and tobacco. After the war the government prosecuted people who tried to avoid these taxes. Other lawsuits were from people who wanted the property the government had taken during the war given back to them. With more federal trials, the government often had to hire private lawyers to handle them all. Some executive departments also hired new lawyers.

Several members of Congress thought the system of hiring outside attorneys was getting too expensive. They didn't like that the attorneys were government employees working in different departments. These lawyers often gave different opinions on a particular legal issue, creating confusion. In 1870 Thomas Jenckes, a representative from Rhode Island, called for the creation of a separate Department of Justice. It would be led by the attorney general. He hoped to end a situation that he said prevented lawyers and citizens from learning "what has been decided, what are the rules governing any department, bureau or officer." The problem, he said, had led to "confusion and conflict." The Judiciary Act of 1870 created the Department of Justice. It also gave the attorney general two assistants and created a new position, the solicitor general.

Solicitors General Who Made History

Benjamin Bristow was named the first U.S. solicitor general in 1870. Almost 50 lawyers have been in the job in the Department of Justice. Several went on to hold even more important government positions. William Howard Taft, the sixth solicitor general, was later elected president of the United States. Archibald Cox is best remembered today for his role in the impeachment process of President Richard Nixon. And several solicitors general became members of the U.S. Supreme Court. The most famous was Thurgood Marshall, who in 1967 became the first African American justice of the Court.

Thurgood Marshall was the first African American to serve on the Supreme Court.

The Judiciary Act of 1870 failed to do two things. It did not give the attorney general and his staff their own offices. The lawyers were spread out across Washington. This made it hard for the AG to work with his staff in the age before telephones and other modern means of communication. The DOJ would not have its own building in Washington, D.C., until 1935. And the law did not eliminate all the lawyers working for other U.S. agencies. They still represented their departments in court. Today individual departments still have their own legal staff. These lawyers mostly give advice on legal issues related only to their own departments.

With the new Department of Justice, the attorney general became the supervisor of U.S. marshals. The original Judiciary Act of 1789 created these positions in the federal government. The marshals serve four-year terms and can hire deputies to help them with their duties. They are responsible for carrying out orders given by federal judges, the president, or Congress. That includes serving subpoenas, which are legal documents that require someone to appear in court. The marshals also arrest suspects and guard prisoners.

U.S. marshals and Atlanta police arrested more than 40 suspected gang members during a raid in 2011.

A Growing Department

As the 20th century began, the Department of Justice was growing. The creation of new divisions and other agencies reflected changes in society. By the early 1900s, the country had grown tremendously. This led to a rise of all sorts of crime, from robbery to political corruption. In 1908 Attorney General Charles J. Bonaparte called for a "force of special agents" to investigate crimes for the DOJ. This is considered the creation of the Federal Bureau of Investigation, though the bureau was not officially named that until several decades later.

Under FBI Director J. Edgar Hoover, the FBI became one of the world's great detective services. It began a national collection of fingerprints to help identify criminals. The FBI also collected records from local law enforcement officials on what types of crimes were committed. The bureau still collects this information today. It helps the FBI see which crimes are most common and what police should focus on.

J. Edgar Hoover ran the FBI from 1924 till his death in 1972.

The FBI gained its biggest fame, however, as it tried to fight the wave of robberies and murders in the 1930s. The bureau had already put out wanted posters, but it also talked about "public enemies" in its office communications. The newspapers then gave the title "Public Enemy Number One" to gangster John Dillinger. He was a bank robber who had broken out of several jails and been involved in deadly shootouts with police. FBI agents eventually shot and killed Dillinger outside a Chicago movie theater in 1934.

While the FBI had the job of catching criminals, another DOJ division tried them in federal courts. The Criminal Division was created in 1919. Over the years, separate units were added to handle certain kinds of crimes The division also played an important part in writing several 1930s laws relating to crime. These laws outlined specific crimes that fell under federal legal investigation. They gave the FBI greater freedom to make arrests and carry weapons. The laws reflected the idea that criminals often operated across state lines and that law enforcement was more of a national issue than ever.

One section in the Criminal Division handles issues related to civil rights. These include such things as the right to vote and to receive a fair trial, regardless of a person's race, religion, or ethnicity. The 1940s and 1950s saw African Americans speak out more forcefully for their civil rights. After the end of slavery in 1865, most black Americans faced decades of legal discrimination across the country and particularly in the South. In 1957 Congress passed the Civil Rights Act. In part, the law created a separate Civil Rights Division in the DOJ to take on cases of discrimination against African Americans and other groups.

WANTED

JOHN HERBERT DILLINGER

On June 23, 1934, HOMER S. CUMMINGS, Attorney General of the United States, under the authority vested in him by an Act of Congress approved June 6, 1934, offered a reward of

$10,000.00

for the capture of John Herbert Dillinger or a reward of

$5,000.00

for information leading to the arrest of John Herbert Dillinger.

DESCRIPTION

Age, 32 years; Height, 5 feet 7-1/8 inches; Weight, 153 pounds; Build, medium; Hair, medium chestnut; Eyes, grey; Complexion, medium; Occupation, machinist; Marks and scars, 1/2 inch scar back left hand, scar middle upper lip, brown mole between eye-brows.

All claims to any of the aforesaid rewards and all questions and disputes that may arise as among claimants to the foregoing rewards shall be passed upon by the Attorney General and his decisions shall be final and conclusive. The right is reserved to divide and allocate portions of any of said rewards as between several claimants. No part of the aforesaid rewards shall be paid to any official or employee of the Department of Justice.

If you are in possession of any information concerning the whereabouts of John Herbert Dillinger, communicate immediately by telephone or telegraph collect to the nearest office of the Division of Investigation, United States Department of Justice, the local addresses of which are set forth on the reverse side of this notice.

JOHN EDGAR HOOVER, DIRECTOR,
DIVISION OF INVESTIGATION,
UNITED STATES DEPARTMENT OF JUSTICE,
WASHINGTON, D. C.

June 25, 1934

Gangster John Dillinger was considered a "public enemy" in 1934.

In the 1960s John Doar led the division. He was respected for his efforts to fight discrimination and protect civil rights. Across the South, state governments made it difficult for black people to register to vote. Young white and black people from across the country rode buses to Mississippi in 1964 to help local black people register to vote. Three of these "Freedom Riders"—Michael Schwerner, Andrew Goodman, and James Chaney—were killed by white racists who opposed their work. In 1967 Doar successfully prosecuted seven of the men arrested for the murders—the first convictions in that state for the killing of a civil rights worker. The Civil Rights Division also took part in the investigation after the 1968 murder of civil rights leader Martin Luther King Jr. The division's work goes on today. It works to fight discrimination on the basis of race, color, sex, disability, religion, and national origin. It also seeks to prevent landlords from discriminating against renters who have children.

Another important division in today's Department of Justice is the Antitrust Division. The division's goal is to stop large businesses from having complete control over the production and sale of a particular product. That effort began in 1890 with the Sherman Antitrust Act. A trust was a business arrangement between companies in the same industry. It created one huge company that controlled almost the entire the industry. The 1890 law tried to weaken the trusts. That work continued in the early 1900s as the Department of Justice filed lawsuits to break up trusts. One of them was the Standard Oil Company, which controlled much of the production of U.S. oil. In 1909 the DOJ took the company to court. Two years later, the U.S. Supreme Court ordered that Standard Oil split into 34 independent companies.

After working for the Department of Justice, John Doar (standing) investigated the Watergate crimes as special counsel for the U.S. House Judiciary Committee.

In 1933 the Justice Department created its Antitrust Division. It works to prevent the joining of companies if the new company's size might lead it to unfairly control a market. The division might also call for a large company to be broken into smaller companies if its size hurts competitors, as with Standard Oil. In 1974 the DOJ filed suit against American Telephone and Telegraph (AT&T). AT&T dominated the country's local phone service. As with the earlier trusts, that size and economic power meant that consumers had to pay higher prices than if many companies competed for their business. After years of legal battles, the company agreed to create new, separate companies to handle local phone service. AT&T could still handle long-distance calls. AT&T was also allowed to make and sell phone equipment and enter into computer data services.

The DOJ's Drug Enforcement Administration (DEA) was also created because of specific problems in the United States. Through the 1960s and early 1970s, national leaders worried about the increasing use of illegal drugs. As part of the War on Drugs, in 1973 President Nixon asked Congress to create one agency within the DOJ to enforce drug laws. Part of that effort included stopping illegal drugs from entering the country from overseas. The DEA also built state-of-the-art labs to test substances to see if they were in fact illegal drugs.

These are just some of the divisions within the DOJ that continue to play a role in enforcing the nation's laws.

Making History

For more than 200 years, the nation's attorney general was a man. President Bill Clinton changed that. In 1993 he named Janet Reno as his attorney general. Clinton had nominated two other women before her. Each had faced questions about hiring undocumented immigrants to work in their homes. Reno held her job for eight years. Before going to Washington, she had served as a Florida state attorney. While Reno served as attorney general, the FBI caught Ted Kaczynski, who was known as the Unabomber. For almost two decades, he sent explosive packages to people across America, killing three and wounding two dozen. The DOJ under Reno also caught and convicted the terrorists who planted bombs under New York's World Trade Center in 1993.

Janet Reno, appointed by President Bill Clinton in 1993, was the nation's first female attorney general.

CHAPTER THREE

Challenges and Change

In October 1973 President Richard Nixon was in a difficult situation. Since that summer he had been fighting a subpoena issued by Archibald Cox. Cox wanted Nixon to turn in secret tape recordings made in the Oval Office, the president's office in the White House. Cox had been named a special prosecutor by Attorney General Elliot Richardson. Cox's job was to learn what part, if any, Nixon had played in a break-in. The burglary had taken place in 1972 at the headquarters of the Democratic National Committee during the presidential campaign.

Did Nixon know about it beforehand? Had he tried to cover up his ties to the burglars after they were caught? Nixon, a Republican, had run for reelection that year and won easily. But now Cox's investigation and one by members of the Senate were making it difficult for the president to govern. And if Cox or the Senate found that Nixon had broken the law, he could be impeached.

Attorney General Elliot Richardson appointed Archibald Cox as special prosecutor to investigate President Nixon's involvement in the Watergate burglary.

Special Prosecutors and the Executive Branch

The U.S. attorney general can name a special prosecutor to take on cases involving members of the executive branch. This is to make sure that the Department of Justice can carry out a fair legal investigation of officials close to the president or others in his administration. President Ulysses S. Grant, through his attorney general, named the first special prosecutor in 1875. He investigated a group of federal officials and others who were stealing tax money owed to the government.

In the 1970s Elliot Richardson became Nixon's third attorney general. The first, John Mitchell, had resigned to run Nixon's 1972 presidential campaign. Mitchell was later sent to prison for approving the money used to carry out the Watergate break-in. His replacement, Richard Kleindienst, resigned in 1973 as the Watergate investigation went on. When he was picked to serve as AG, Richardson promised he would name a special prosecutor to investigate the case. Several years later, Congress passed a law that created the position of the independent counsel. This lawyer would play a similar role as past special prosecutors. He or she would investigate possible illegal actions by members of the executive branch. Three judges would choose this person after the attorney general called for it. The law creating the independent counsel is no longer in effect. The attorney general can still name someone to be a special counsel with similar duties.

Under U.S. law, a special counsel is called for when the attorney general or acting attorney general finds that it is necessary to criminally investigate a person or matter. A special counsel helps avoid a conflict of interest. It can also be in the best interest of the public.

Special Prosecutor Archibald Cox answered questions from reporters after his firing was announced.

The Watergate Scandal

The June 1972 break-in was at a Washington, D.C., office, apartment, and hotel complex called the Watergate. Soon that name—Watergate—was used to describe the scandal that was unfolding around Nixon. In May 1973 Congress began to investigate the activities of people who worked with Nixon. That October the sense that Nixon had done something illegal grew when he ordered Richardson to fire Cox. The attorney general refused and resigned. His deputy AG, William Ruckelshaus, also refused to carry out Nixon's order. He resigned too. Solicitor General Robert Bork finally did as Nixon wished and fired Cox. All this activity took place on a Saturday night. It was later nicknamed "the Saturday Night Massacre." The president's actions brought harsh criticism from lawmakers in both parties.

Marchers in Boston called for President Nixon's impeachment in 1973.

Writing years after the Saturday Night Massacre, Richardson explained why he would not fire Cox. "'The more I thought about it, the clearer it seemed to me that public confidence in the investigation would depend on its being independent not only in fact, but in appearance." That independent search for the truth would be destroyed if he did what the president ordered. But Nixon had his own strong feelings about the subpoena and how the situation played out. Cox had refused the president's order to drop the subpoena seeking the tapes. To Nixon the tapes were records of private presidential communication. He thought he had no legal duty to release them. Cox was technically a member of the executive branch, and Nixon believed he should have followed the president's order. Nixon wrote, "Clearly the government of the United States cannot function if employees of the executive branch are free to ignore in this fashion the instructions of the President."

The new special prosecutor was Leon Jaworski. He continued to press for the release of Nixon's White House tapes. The case ended up in the Supreme Court. It ruled in July 1974 that the president had to turn them over. By then the House of Representatives was already holding hearings to decide if it should impeach the president. Rather than face a probable impeachment, Nixon resigned.

Political and Legal Relationships

The Watergate scandal was the most extreme example of the pressures the attorney general and the Department of Justice face. On one hand, the attorney general is part of the president's cabinet. The AG has a political duty to carry out the president's policies as part of the executive branch. On the other hand, attorneys general and their staffs are supposed to uphold the law and carry out prosecutions when needed. That includes investigating other members of the executive branch, the president's closest associates, or the president. Former attorney general Edward Levi said that AGs must have "a proper loyalty which we all recognize as lawyers to the idea of law itself."

More than 10,000 Japanese Americans were incarcerated at the Manzanar internment camp in California between 1942 and 1945.

The tension within the Justice Department over its dual roles is not new. Several attorneys general have wrestled with what they thought was legal versus what the president wanted. In 1941 Japan attacked the U.S. naval base at Pearl Harbor, Hawaii. Soon after, some military advisers and newspapers wanted the president to relocate people of Japanese ancestry, including ones who were U.S. citizens, away from the West Coast. Many Japanese Americans lived along the coast. Some officials believed they might not be loyal to the United States. U.S. leaders also believed that if Japan attacked the United States again, it would attack that region first. Attorney General Francis Biddle was against moving the Japanese who were citizens. He thought the government could legally move citizens of Japan who were living in the United States, since the U.S. and Japan were at war. U.S. citizens of Japanese background had more legal rights. He also argued that the FBI had not found any evidence that the Japanese who lived in the U.S. were a major threat to the country.

President Franklin D. Roosevelt, however, sided with his secretary of war, who called for moving all people of Japanese ancestry away from the coast. When the president made his decision, Biddle went along with it. The DOJ ran some of the camps where the Japanese were jailed. Throughout the war Biddle's Department of Justice fought any legal challenge to the president's power to deny the legal rights of U.S. citizens with Japanese roots. In one case the solicitor general seemed to ignore information that weakened the government's argument about the dangers Japanese Americans posed.

Attorney General Francis Biddle enforced President Roosevelt's orders to incarcerate Japanese Americans during World War II.

Conflicts of Interest

In recent years, attorneys general have sometimes approved or carried out presidential policies that did not violate the Constitution but did violate laws. That can lead to what is called a conflict of interest. Can the attorney general be counted on to do a fair investigation when he or she has been so involved in the political process that it raises legal questions?

That question arose in 1986 and 1987, with the so-called Iran-Contra scandal. Foreign affairs thousands of miles apart came together in this affair. The administration of President Ronald Reagan was trying to solve two problems at once. It wanted to arm Nicaraguan rebels, called Contras, who were fighting the government in Nicaragua. That government denied its citizens freedom of speech and locked up people who opposed its policies. Congress, though, had passed a law making it illegal to provide the rebels with military aid. Reagan also wanted to win the release of Americans kidnapped by terrorist groups backed by Iran. Members of the executive branch came up with a plan to sell U.S. weapons to Iran secretly even though the United States had earlier forbidden it. Then the administration would use the money from the weapons sales to aid the Contras in Nicaragua even though the law prohibited this.

The attorney general at the time was Edwin Meese. It was alleged that he knew about the arms deal with Iran before it became public. It was also alleged that he knew it was illegal. But he did not know about the money going to the Contras. Some legal experts argued that Meese should have recused, or taken himself out of, the investigation that began in November 1986. His efforts to uncover what happened and whether laws were broken were not very thorough. He didn't take notes when he questioned several top executive branch officials. Meese also made public statements about the deal that turned out to be not true. Some legal experts believed the attorney general was more interested in protecting Reagan's reputation than learning the truth.

Another attorney general who faced controversy had almost no relationship with the president when taking the office. In 1993 Janet Reno was not President Bill Clinton's first choice for attorney general. The two had not worked together before. Reno was put into the public eye in the spring of that year. She had approved the FBI's plan to address a problem with a religious group in Waco, Texas. The group, called the Branch Davidians, was known to have illegal weapons stored in their compound. Government officials also believed children in the group were being physically and sexually abused. Reno said the FBI could try to drive the group

In an attempt to save victims of a dangerous religious leader, Janet Reno approved an FBI raid of their compound in Waco, Texas, in 1993.

out of their compound by using tear gas. The plan failed. Members of the group started fires that spread rapidly and destroyed the compound. More than 80 Branch Davidians were killed. The failed raid made some lawmakers question Reno's judgment. Reno had often said she was going to let facts dictate her actions, not politics. In the end, she refused to appoint independent counsels when she didn't think there was a legal reason to. That was the case when some Republicans thought Vice President Al Gore broke the law while raising campaign money in 1996. Reno believed the Justice Department could fairly investigate the charges. However, according to legal scholar David Yalof, Reno's decisions "made enemies of both Republicans and Democrats."

Shortly after Clinton left the White House in 2001, President George W. Bush and his new attorney general faced a major crisis. On September 11 of that year, terrorists struck the United States. They took control of four airplanes and used them to carry out attacks. Two planes crashed into the twin towers of New York City's World Trade Center. A third plane crashed into the Pentagon, the headquarters of the U.S. military. The fourth plane crashed in a Pennsylvania field before it could reach the terrorists' likely planned target in Washington, D.C. The attacks killed almost 3,000 people.

Soon after the 9/11 attack, divisions within the Department of Justice worked on finding out more about the terrorists and people who helped them carry out their plot. The FBI had a major role in this. Its agents examined the crime scenes, which were the largest the bureau had ever dealt with. They took in hundreds of thousands of tips about the terrorists and possible future attacks. In the years after 9/11, the DOJ prosecuted terrorists who plotted to carry out more attacks on the United States or overseas targets.

In the fight against terrorism, the attorney general and some DOJ officials seemed to support government tactics that were illegal, or at least questionable. Attorney General John Ashcroft supported the Patriot Act of 2001. It gave the government new powers to secretly collect information on Americans. But Ashcroft and others in the DOJ pushed back when Bush wanted to carry out more secret surveillance of suspected terrorists. Ashcroft and the others thought this was illegal. They threatened to resign when Bush said he was going to carry them out anyway. The president backed down. But Bush later introduced security measures that collected Internet messages from millions of people.

Former Missouri governor John Ashcroft was appointed attorney general in 2001 by President George W. Bush.

The Bush administration also wanted to question suspected terrorists using methods that some people considered torture, which is illegal. Lawyers in one department of the DOJ wrote that the policies the administration wanted to pursue were legal. Attorney General Ashcroft supported these lawyers. However, many people inside and outside the government thought the techniques Ashcroft approved amounted to illegal torture.

As these examples show, the battle against terrorism sometimes put the Department of Justice in a difficult position. It wanted to give the executive branch broad powers to prevent future attacks. But at times that has led DOJ officials to support policies that some critics questioned.

Fighting New Kinds of Crime

The FBI has played a major role in the Justice Department's efforts to fight terrorism and other types of crimes that have become more common. In 2005 the bureau created the National Security Branch. One part of that is the Counterterrorism Division. Its role is to fight terrorism around the world. It works with other U.S. government agencies and at times with foreign governments. The division has people who speak many languages. Some agents in the division also look for where the terrorists get money to pay for their activities. Another recent concern of the FBI has been cybercrime—using the Internet to carry out illegal acts. In some cases cybercriminals might want to steal money from online bank accounts. In other cases terrorists might use the Internet to stop services at a power plant, hospital, or government office. As in the fight against terrorism, FBI agents in the Cyber Division work with other U.S. agencies and operate around the world.

CHAPTER FOUR

Justice Today and Tomorrow

On a sunny afternoon in September 2017, several hundred high school and college students in Albuquerque, New Mexico, left their classrooms. They met on city streets to protest a change in U.S. law enforcement. That day, Attorney General Jeff Sessions had announced what many people expected: The administration of President Donald Trump would not support the Deferred Action for Childhood Arrivals (DACA) program. President Barack Obama had put the program in place in 2012. It was created to help young Americans who had been brought into the United States without documentation by their immigrant parents. These young people were called "Dreamers."

Dreamers was a reference to a law that would give these young people legal status in the United States. "Dreamers" also meant that the young people wanted

Demonstrators in Washington, D.C., protested President Trump's decision to end DACA, a program to help children of undocumented immigrants.

to pursue the American Dream: having the chance to develop their talents, then use them to have a successful career. Like most Americans the young people wanted to be able to start families, own homes, and contribute to their communities. Obama and others did not think these young people should be penalized because their parents brought them into the country when they were children. Obama did not want to send the Dreamers back to countries they had no memories of. For them, the United States was their home.

Congress did not pass the law that would protect the Dreamers and let them stay in the country. So Obama ordered the Department of Homeland Security—whose mission is to secure the nation from threats—not to search for or arrest the young immigrants if they were not breaking any U.S. laws.

Attorney General Jeff Sessions, appointed by President Donald Trump, sided with Trump on the issue of ending DACA.

In 2014 Obama's Justice Department had determined that the federal government had the right to make arresting undocumented immigrants other than the Dreamers a priority. DACA let about 800,000 young immigrants, most from Mexico and Central America, go to school, work, and raise families without fear of being arrested. One student at the Albuquerque rally said that DACA let him legally work at a local fast-food restaurant. His goal was to finish high school and study to become an engineer. "That's my dream right now," he said. But with the changes announced by Sessions, he said, "I'm not sure if it's going to happen."

Sessions argued that Obama and his administration had violated the Constitution when it put DACA in place. In the new attorney general and President Trump's interpretation of the Constitution, only Congress could set immigration policy. Trump had made illegal immigration a key part of his campaign for president. He proposed building a wall along the entire border with Mexico. He called for deporting even more undocumented immigrants already in the country. His Justice Department's interpretation of DACA reflected his desire to stop illegal immigration. Supporters of DACA, however, believed Obama did have the right to prioritize which undocumented people to deport. They also thought that the Dreamers should not be punished for something their parents did—breaking the law by bringing them into the country when they were children.

Presidential Focus

The DACA issue was just one example of how the DOJ can change which laws it focuses on depending on a president's policy goals. Once Congress passes a law, it remains in force unless the Supreme Court finds it unconstitutional or Congress changes it later on. But the executive branch, acting through the Justice Department, has the power to enforce some laws more actively than others. Individual presidents can also shape policy by their executive orders. Before these are issued, the DOJ's Office of Legal Counsel reviews if they are legal or not. But as the torture controversy during the Bush administration showed, legal experts can disagree on what is or isn't legal.

Trump was elected as a Republican. Many of his views differed greatly from Obama's, who was a Democrat. Whether or not to protect Dreamers was just one difference in the two men's political beliefs. In every administration, the DOJ might make arguments for or against certain legal positions when a case involving state laws ends up in federal courts. This usually happens when a state law might violate federal law or the Constitution.

The Trump Justice Department also took an opposing view from the Obama administration on rights for gay and lesbian Americans. In 2014 Obama's attorney general Eric Holder wrote that the federal government would defend the rights of people in the workplace regardless of their sexual identity. That included the rights of transgender people—people who were assigned one gender at birth and identify as another. The DOJ also reviewed a ruling by the Equal Employment Opportunity Commission (EEOC). The EEOC is part of the executive branch. It can sue if a company discriminates against workers. In 2015 the EEOC under Obama ruled that discriminating against someone because of their sexual orientation was illegal.

Under the Trump administration, the Department of Justice took the unusual step of taking sides in a discrimination case between two private parties. A worker sued his company after it fired him for being gay. The case reached the U.S. Court of Appeals. The administration argued that the law in question did not offer legal protection to someone who was fired because of his or her sexual orientation. The law was Title VII of the Civil Rights Act of 1964. Critics of the department's involvement in the case saw it as a part of larger government effort under Trump to deny gay, lesbian, and transgender people legal protection.

The Civil Rights Act of 1964

Title VII was just one part of the Civil Rights Act of 1964. Here's a look at other parts of the law and what they address.

Title I
Voting rights

Title II
Discrimination in public places

Title III
Segregation in public places

Title IV
Segregation in public schools

Title V
The Civil Rights Commission and how it functions

Title VI
Discrimination by government agencies that receive federal money

Title VII
Equal employment opportunities

Title VIII
Collection of voting statistics

Title IX
Review of judicial action in civil rights cases

Title X
Creation of the Community Relation Service to help settle discrimination disputes in local communities

Title XI
Various legal considerations that could arise from enforcing the law

President Trump came to the White House promising to be tougher on crime than he said President Obama had been. Stepping up enforcement of immigration laws was one of his actions. The DOJ was also concerned about the rise in violent crime, especially murders, in some parts of the country. Some of the violence was connected to gangs. Attorney General Sessions said he wanted to help law enforcement make local streets safer. Some of that work is done through the FBI's Violent Gang Task Force. It works with 170 state and local task forces across the country to address gang violence. In 2018 Trump signed a law that directed the DOJ to give $50 million to local law enforcement agencies to reduce violent crime.

Arming the Police

Attorney General Jeff Sessions wanted to give police all the tools available to fight crime. In 2017 another Obama administration policy was reversed. Under Obama the Department of Justice had found that the use of military-type weapons by local police added to distrust between African American communities and mostly white local police forces. The use of military equipment, Obama said, "can sometimes give people a feeling like there's an occupying force."

His administration began to study the issue in 2014. That year in Ferguson, Missouri, rioters took to the streets after police in the city shot and killed an unarmed black man. In response, the Ferguson police used vehicles and other equipment originally made for the U.S. military. Obama placed limits on the kind of military equipment police could use in the future. Under President Trump, however, the Justice Department ended the limits. Sessions said lifting the ban would give police the equipment they needed to do their jobs. He said it would also "send a strong message that we will not allow criminal activity, violence, and lawlessness to become the new norm."

Avoiding Conflicts of Interest

Changes in Department of Justice policies and attitudes are common when one political party replaces another in the White House. As shown here, the parties and the presidents who lead them can have very different opinions on how to enforce the country's laws. One thing that stays the same is trying to avoid a conflict of interest. Attorneys general are expected to recuse themselves from certain cases if they are seen as being personally involved in some way. In 2012 Eric Holder recused himself from a case about the leaking of government information to journalists. The FBI had questioned him about the leaks. Holder believed that since he had had contact with many journalists, he should not be involved in investigating how reporters received secret government information. He also wanted to ensure that any investigation of members of the executive branch who might have leaked was done fairly.

Eric Holder, appointed by President Barack Obama in 2009, was the first African American attorney general.

President Trump's Attorney General also chose recusal in a DOJ investigation. During the 2016 presidential campaign, Jeff Sessions had been one of Donald Trump's first advisors. After the election, reports appeared that Russia had tried to influence the election. Because of that, Sessions recused himself from a DOJ investigation into the relationship between the Trump presidential campaign and the Russians. In May 2017 Deputy Attorney General Rod Rosenstein appointed a special counsel to find the facts about the Russians' ties to the Trump campaign.

President Trump was angry about both the recusal and the naming of the special counsel. He feared that the Russia investigation could affect his ability to govern as he wanted. But Sessions had done what attorneys general had often done in the past. He wanted to show Americans that the Department of Justice would fairly enforce the law.

Deputy Attorney General Rod Rosenstein appointed Special Counsel Robert Mueller to investigate whether crimes were committed during the 2016 presidential election campaign.

Should Americans Elect the Attorney General?

Being both a political advisor and a key player in enforcing laws has often put U.S. attorneys general in difficult positions. Some legal experts have said one way to lessen the political nature of the job is for Americans to elect the attorney general. That's already the case in most states, and supporters of the idea say the election process makes the AG more independent from the head of the executive branch. That independence would make it easier for the attorney general to carry out investigations of executive branch officials or others who are close to the chief executive—whether it's a governor or the president. In recent years the idea of electing the attorney general has come up while both Democrats and Republicans have controlled the White House. Writing in 2017, retired federal judge Bruce J. Einhorn outlined the value of having an attorney general with greater independence from the White House. He or she could more strongly defend the work of Justice Department officials to fairly carry out investigations of anyone in government accused of breaking the law. Making the AG "the people's lawyer," Einhorn wrote, "will . . . truly ensure 'liberty and justice for all.'"

What You Can Do

If you're concerned about an issue that involves the Department of Justice, you can write the lawmakers who represent you in Congress. Congress often holds meetings to question DOJ officials on their policies, and the lawmakers can sometimes influence what the DOJ does. This link will help you find the member of the House of Representatives for where you live:

https://www.house.gov/representatives/find-your-representative

This link shows the current members of the U.S. Senate. Each state has two senators:

https://www.senate.gov/senators/contact/

Timeline

1789
Congress passes the Judiciary Act, which creates the position of U.S. attorney general; Edmund Randolph is the first person to fill the role.

1870
Congress creates the Department of Justice, with the attorney general leading it.

1875
The Department of Justice names the first special prosecutor to investigate possible criminal acts in the executive branch.

1908
The Department of Justice creates what will become the Federal Bureau of Investigation (FBI).

1919
The Department of Justice creates the Criminal Division.

1933
The Department of Justice creates the Antitrust Division.

1935
The DOJ gets its own office building for the first time.

1957
The department creates the Civil Rights Division.

1973

The Drug Enforcement Agency is created as part of the DOJ; with the so-called Saturday Night Massacre, Attorney General Elliot Richardson and his deputy resign, rather than follow President Richard Nixon's order to fire a special prosecutor investigating Nixon.

1986

Attorney General Edwin Meese is criticized for how he handled the Iran-Contra affair.

1993

President Bill Clinton names Janet Reno the first female attorney general.

2009

President Barack Obama names Eric Holder the first African American attorney general,

2012

President Barack Obama offers some legal protection to young undocumented immigrants through a program known as DACA.

2017

Attorney general Jeff Sessions announces President Donald Trump's plan to end DACA.

2018

The DOJ receives money to give to local law enforcement agencies to fight violent crime.

Glossary

administration—the people who serve a president in the executive branch

appeal—a legal action taken to ask another court to hear the facts of a case already settled by a lower court

civil—relating to legal disputes between private citizens or companies

corruption—illegal acts taken to gain power or money

discrimination—treating someone unfairly because of their race, religion, or other trait

executive—relating to the branch of government that carries out, or executes, laws

federal—relating to the national government of a country

gender—a person's relationship with masculinity, femininity, both, or neither, based on different factors

impeached—removed from a political office for committing illegal acts

incarcerate—to put in prison

intelligence—information gathered secretly about an enemy or foreign country

leaking—releasing important government information without permission

prosecuting—bringing legal charges against someone in court

recuse—to remove oneself from involvement in a legal case

segregation—the separation of people into different groups based on their race or other trait, with one group receiving better treatment than another

surveillance—close observation of a person, especially someone suspected of being a criminal

Additional Resources

Critical Thinking

1. Which officials in the Justice Department can represent the U.S. government in cases that reach the U.S. Supreme Court?

2. Do you think it's a good or bad idea for the Department of Justice to have the power to break up large companies, as it did with AT&T? Explain your reasoning.

3. Why does the Department of Justice sometimes change which laws it chooses to enforce most strictly? What is one example in the book of a difference between one administration's attitude toward a particular law and another's?

Further Reading

Adams, Ashely. *Standing in the Attorney General's Shoes.* New York: Cavendish Square Publishing, 2018.

Braun, Eric. *Loretta Lynch: First African American Woman Attorney General.* Minneapolis: Lerner Publications, 2016.

Fremon, David K. *The Watergate Scandal in United States History.* Berkeley Heights, NJ: Enslow Publishers, Inc., 2015.

Zullo, Allan. *FBI Heroes.* New York: Scholastic Inc., 2015.

Internet Sites

Use Facthound to find Internet sites related to this book.

Visit www.facthound.com

Just type in 9780756559038 and go.

Source Notes

p. 4, "I started seeing..." Gulfstream Goodwill Industries, May 12, 2016. https://www.facebook.com/GulfstreamGoodwill/videos/1110267242348506/ Accessed on September 12, 2018.

p. 15, "To enforce the law and defend the interests... Attorneys General of the United States. The United States Department of Justice. https://www.justice.gov/about Accessed on September 12, 2018.

p. 19, "Learned in the law...prosecute and conduct..." The Judiciary Act, September 24, 1789. The Avalon Project, Yale Law School. http://avalon.law.yale.edu/18th_century/judiciary_act.asp Accessed on September 12, 2018.

p. 19, "I have considered the first arrangement..." George Washington to Edmund Randolph, September 28, 1789. Library of Congress. https://www.loc.gov/resource/mgw2.022/?sp=177&st=text Accessed on September 12, 2018.

p. 22, "What has been decided...confusion and conflict" Nancy V. Baker, *Conflicting Loyalties: Law and Politics in the Attorney General's Office*, 1789-1990 (Lawrence: University Press of Kansas, 1992), p. 62.

p. 25, "Force of special agents" "The Nation Calls, 1908-1923," History of the FBI, https://www.fbi.gov/history/brief-history Accessed on September 12, 2018.

p. 37, "The more I thought about it..." Neil A. Lewis, "Elliot Richardson Dies at 79; Stood Up to Nixon and Resigned In 'Saturday Night Massacre.'" *The New York Times*, January 1, 2000. http://www.nytimes.com/learning/general/onthisday/bday/0720.html Accessed on September 12, 2018.

p. 37, "Clearly the government of the United States..." Carroll Kilpatrick, "Nixon Forces Firing of Cox; Richardson, Ruckelshaus Quit President Abolishes Prosecutor's Office; FBI Seals Records." *The Washington Post*, October 21, 1973. http://www.washingtonpost.com/wp-srv/national/longterm/watergate/articles/102173-2.htm Accessed on September 12, 2018.

p. 37, "A proper loyalty which we all recognize..." *Conflicting Loyalties*, p. 3.

p. 42, "Made enemies of both Republicans and Democrats." David Alistair Yalof, *Prosecution Among Friends: President, Attorney General, and Executive Branch Wrongdoing.* (College Station: Texas A & M Press, 2012), p. 140.

p. 48, "That's my dream right now..." Kim Burgess, "Hundreds of New Mexico Students 'Walk Out' Over DACA Decision." *Albuquerque Journal*, September 5, 2017. https://www.abqjournal.com/1058642/new-mexico-students-plan-walk-out-over-daca-decision.html Accessed on September 12, 2018.

p. 52, "Can sometimes give people a feeling..." Trymaine, Lee, "Obama to Ban Military Weapons Sent to "Local Police Departments." MSNBC, July 21, 2015. http://www.msnbc.com/msnbc/obama-ban-military-weapons-sent-local-police-departments Accessed on September 12, 2018.

p. 52, "Send a strong message that we will not allow..." Pete Williams and Julia Ainsley. "Trump Reverses Obama Policy on Surplus Military Gear for Police." NBC News, August 28, 2017.

p. 56, "The people's lawyer...will...truly ensure..." Bruce J. Einhorn, "Time to Let the American People Elect the US Attorney General." The Hill, June 20, 2017. http://thehill.com/blogs/pundits-blog/the-administration/338536-its-time-we-let-the-american-people-elect-the-us Accessed on September 12, 2018.

Select Bibliography

Attorneys General of the United States. The United States Department of Justice. https://www.justice.gov/about Accessed on September 12, 2018.

Back to a Future Initiative. Palm Beach County, Public Safety – Justice Services. http://discover.pbcgov.org/publicsafety/justiceservices/Reentry/BacktoFuture.aspx
Accessed on September 12, 2018.

Baker, Nancy V. *Conflicting Loyalties: Law and Politics in the Attorney General's Office*, 1789-1990. Lawrence: University Press of Kansas, 1992.

Burgess, Kim. "Hundreds of New Mexico Students 'Walk Out' Over DACA Decision." *Albuquerque Journal*, September 5, 2017. https://www.abq-journal.com/1058642/new-mexico-students-plan-walk-out-over-daca-decision.html
Accessed on September 12, 2018.

Cummings, William. "Special Counsel vs. Special Prosecutor: What's the Difference?" *USA Today*, May 17, 2017. https://www.usatoday.com/story/news/politics/onpolitics/2017/05/18/special-counsel-vs-special-prosecutor-difference/329016001/
Accessed on September 12, 2018.

Department of Justice websites, including:
The Department of Justice
https://www.justice.gov/

The Federal Bureau of Investigation
https://www.fbi.gov/

Offices of the United States Attorneys
https://www.justice.gov/usao
Accessed on September 12, 2018.

Einhorn, Bruce J. "Time to Let the American People Elect the US Attorney General." The Hill, June 20, 2017. http://thehill.com/blogs/pundits-blog/the-administration/338536-its-time-we-let-the-american-people-elect-the-us
Accessed on September 12, 2018.

Hulse, Carl. "Janet Reno, First Woman to Serve as U.S. Attorney General, Dies at 78." *The New York Times*, November 7, 2016. https://www.nytimes.com/2016/11/08/us/janet-reno-dead.html
Accessed on September 12, 2018.

The Judiciary Act, September 24, 1789. The Avalon Project, Yale Law School. http://avalon.law.yale.edu/18th_century/judiciary_act.asp
Accessed on September 12, 2018.

"The Nation Calls, 1908-1923." History of the FBI. https://www.fbi.gov/history/brief-history
Accessed on September 12, 2018.

Robinson, Nick. "Elect, Don't Appoint, the US Attorney General." *Christian Science Monitor*, January 30, 2009. https://www.csmonitor.com/Commentary/Opinion/2009/0130/p09s01-coop.html Accessed on September 12, 2018.

Second Chance Act Grant Program. The National Reentry Resource Center, https://csgjusticecenter.org/nrrc/projects/second-chance-act/
Accessed on September 12, 2018.

Thaler, Cynthia, and Katy Albis. "Palm Beach County Program Partners With Probation Officers to Improve Reentry, One Youth at a Time." The National Reentry Resource Center, September 13, 2017. https://csgjusticecenter.org/nrrc/posts/palm-beach-county-program-partners-with-probation-officers-to-improve-reentry-one-youth-at-a-time/ Accessed on September 12, 2018.

Williams, Pete, and Julia Ainsley. "Trump Reverses Obama Policy on Surplus Military Gear for Police." NBC News, August 28, 2017.

Yalof, David Alistair. *Prosecution Among Friends: President, Attorney General, and Executive Branch Wrongdoing.* College Station: Texas A & M Press, 2012.

Index

About the Author

Michael Burgan has written numerous books for children and young adults during his nearly 25 years as a freelance writer. Many of his books have focused on U.S. history, geography, and the lives of world leaders. Michael has won several awards for his writing; and his graphic novel version of the classic tale *Frankenstein* (Stone Arch Books) was a Junior Library Guild selection. Michael graduated from the University of Connecticut with a bachelor's degree in history. He lives in Santa Fe, New Mexico, with his cat, Callie.